Pup and Hound's Big Book of Stories

Written by

Susan Hood

Illustrated by

Linda Hendry

Kids Can Press

✿ Kids Can Read ® Kids Can Read is a registered trademark of Kids Can Press Ltd.

Pup and Hound's Big Book of Stories: A Collection of 6 First Readers
Text © 2014 Susan Hood
Illustrations © 2014 Linda Hendry

This book includes the following stories:
Pup and Hound, first published in 2004
Pup and Hound Move In, first published in 2004
Pup and Hound Stay Up Late, first published in 2005
Pup and Hound in Trouble, first published in 2005
Pup and Hound Play Copycats, first published in 2007
Pup and Hound Hatch an Egg, first published in 2007

Kids Can Press acknowledges the financial support of the Government of
Ontario, through the Ontario Media Development Corporation's Ontario Book
Initiative; the Ontario Arts Council; the Canada Council for the Arts; and the
Government of Canada, through the CBF, for our publishing activity.

Published in Canada by   Published in the U.S. by
Kids Can Press Ltd.   Kids Can Press Ltd.
25 Dockside Drive   2250 Military Road
Toronto, ON M5A 0B5   Tonawanda, NY 14150

www.kidscanpress.com

Edited by Tara Walker and Yvette Ghione

This book is smyth sewn casebound.
Manufactured in Shenzhen, China, in 10/2013 by C & C Offset

CM 14 0 9 8 7 6 5 4 3 2 1

Library and Archives Canada Cataloguing in Publication

Hood, Susan [Novels. Selections]
    Pup and hound's big book of stories : a collection of 6 first
readers / written by Susan Hood ; illustrated by Linda Hendry.

(Kids Can read)
Contents: Pup and hound — Pup and hound move in — Pup and
    hound stay up late — Pup and hound in trouble — Pup and
    hound play copycats — Pup and hound hatch an egg.

For ages 5–6.
ISBN 978-1-77138-121-5 (bound)

    I. Hendry, Linda, illustrator II. Title. III. Series: Kids Can
read (Toronto, Ont.)

PZ7.H758Pubi 2014   j813'.54   C2013-905728-5

Kids Can Press is a *LORUS*™ Entertainment company

Contents

Pup and Hound

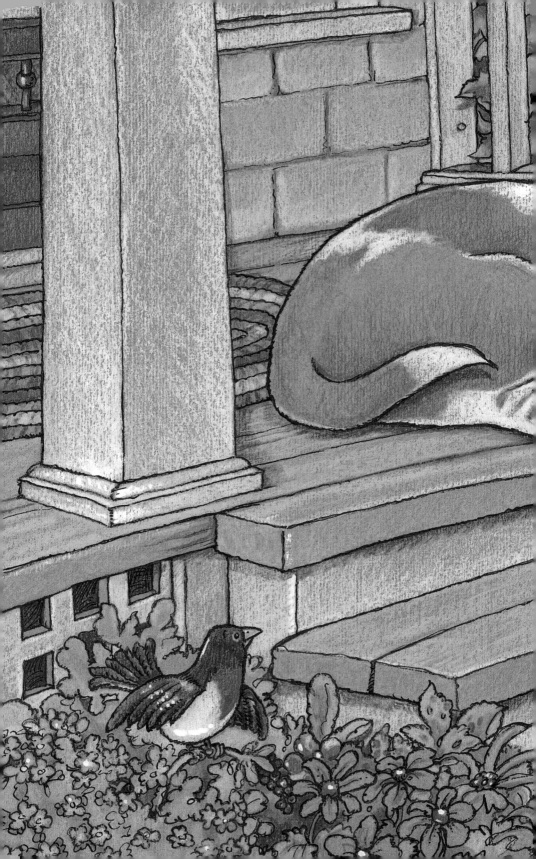

What was that?

What was that sound?

Hound looked around.

He sniffed the ground

until he found ...

... what made that sound!

It was small and round,

curled on the ground.

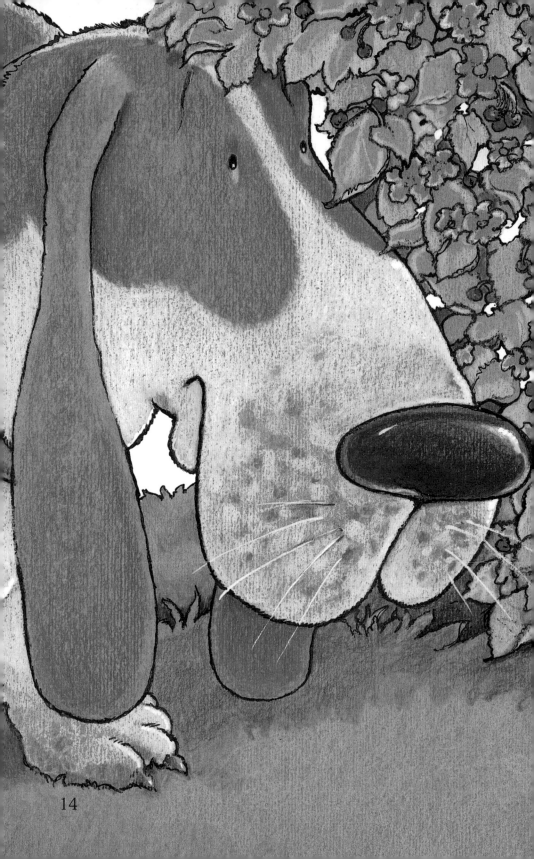

14

It was Pup.

He was fed up!

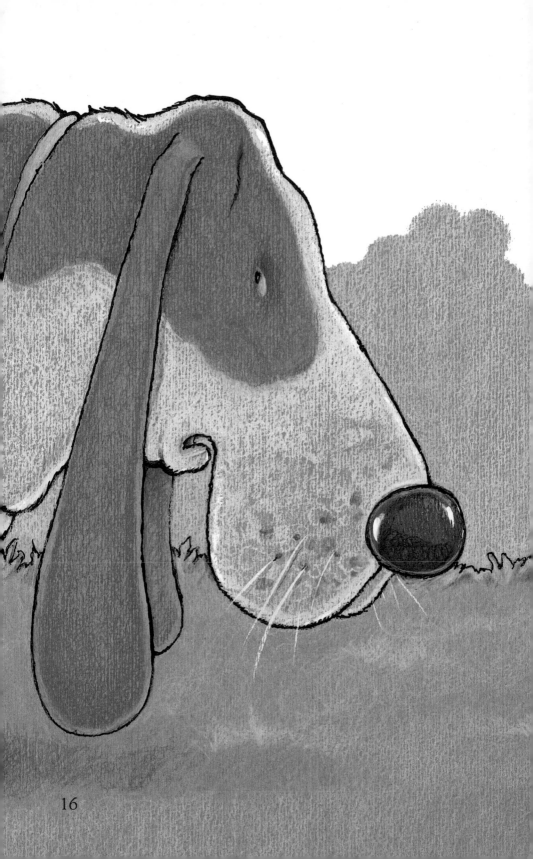

"Bow wow wow!"

said Pup to Hound.

"I want to eat —

now, now, now!"

Hound looked around

until he found ...

a stick!

Ick!

A shoe?

Ewww!

A bone?

Groan!

Then Hound found
a treat to eat.

Meat!

Neat!

Pup gobbled up

all the meat.

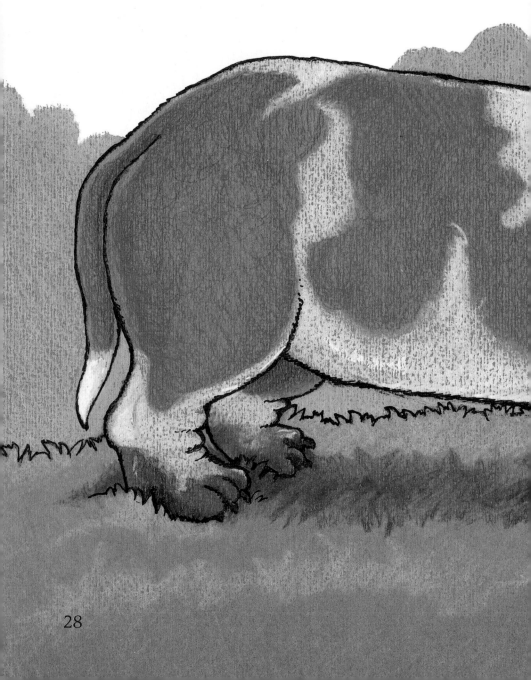

He left nothing

for poor Hound to eat!

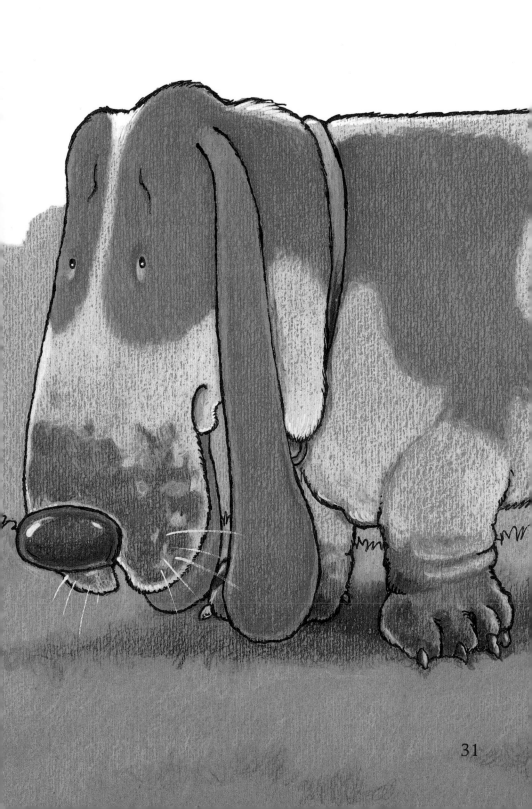

Never mind.

Hound chewed the stick.

Then Hound gave Pup

a goodnight lick.

Pup and Hound
Move In

What was that?

What woke Hound up?

It was near dawn —

Yawn!

What woke Hound up?

It was Pup!

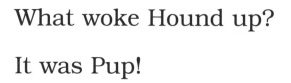

Pup came over

every day.

"Woof! Woof!" he'd say.

"Come out and play!"

They played follow-the-leader
and tug-of-war.

And Hound wasn't lonely

anymore.

At night, Pup went home

to his old boot bed.

He wished he was

somewhere else instead.

Pup didn't want

to live alone.

So he left with

everything he owned.

His good friend Hound

took him in

and promised to

take care of him.

But the day Pup moved in,

he took Hound's bone.

Groan!

He ate Hound's food.

How rude!

He slept in Hound's bed!

Sleepyhead!

Hound stretched out on

the hard wood floor.

And then — oh, no!

That puppy snored!

When Hound woke up,

Pup wasn't there.

Hound found him

with his special bear.

Pup was teething,

as puppies do.

He needed to chew

and chew and chew!

Hound grabbed his bear.

And Pup did, too.

They pulled and pulled!

Bear split in two!

The pigs and cows

stopped to stare.

They knew it was

Hound's special bear.

Even the donkeys

looked up from their hay.

Hound sighed, turned

and walked away.

Pup heard a howl,

a low, sad song.

Other dogs heard

and howled along.

Pup crept up the hill
without a sound.
He gave his
lucky sock to Hound.

Then Pup howled, too,

"Ah-rut-ah-rooooooooooooo!"

It sounded so funny,

what could Hound do?

Hound wagged his tail.

Pup wagged his, too.

Then Hound found something
for Pup to chew.

Pup and Hound Stay Up Late

What was that?

It wasn't Pup.

It was late.

Who woke Hound up?

Hound saw something —

a long, thin snout.

"Grrr," he growled.

"Grrr! Get out."

The very next night,

Hound woke up again.

He looked around.

Where was his friend?

Where was Pup

at this late hour?

"Woof!" There he was

beside the flowers.

Hound marched Pup

back home to bed.

But Pup had other ideas instead.

When Hound was asleep,

Pup tiptoed out

to meet a friend

with a long, thin snout.

They made a plan

to meet each night.

They played kick the can — *BAM!* —

and chased moonlight.

They played tag —

and freeze!

They just hung around.

But when the sun came up,

Pup fell down.

Mother doves cooed,

"Poor dear! Sleepyhead!"

Mockingbirds cried,

"Silly Pup! Go to bed!"

Hound woke up later.

He heard Pup snore.

Pup slept ...

and slept ...

and slept some more.

Hound grunted and sighed.

What was wrong with Pup?

He was sleeping all day!

Would he ever get up?

That night, Hound saw

a long, thin snout.

He saw Pup get up

and followed him out.

Who was Pup with?

Hound had to know.

Was it a fox?

Or a rat? Oh, no!

Silly old Hound!

What's wrong? What's up?

It's just Otto —

Otto and Pup!

Otto, the opossum,

was fuzzy and round.

He scooted over

and nuzzled Hound.

"Play with us, Hound!

Let's stay up!"

So Hound hung out

with Otto and Pup.

Next day, their friends
all gathered around.
What was the matter
with Pup and Hound?

Pup and Hound in Trouble

What was that?

What was that yelp?

Uh-oh! Oh, no!

Pup needs help!

Pup scooted from

his muddy bath.

Hound pulled him from

the horse's path!

Yuck! What a mess!

Time to clean up.

But when a frog jumped ...

... so did Pup!

Pup swam and swam.

"Yip, yap! Yip, yelp!"

Uh-oh! Oh, no!

Pup needs help!

Pup was stuck

in weeds and muck.

"Quack! Quack! Quack!"

cried Mama Duck.

Hound paddled out

to rescue Pup.

He huffed and puffed

and pulled him up.

Pup shook and watered

all the flowers.

"YEOW!" said Cat,

who hated showers.

"Honk-honk! Honk-honk!"

"Yip, yap! Yip, yelp!"

Uh-oh! Oh, no!

Pup needs help!

Hound dashed in

and stood his ground.

But Pup was gone

when he turned around.

"Oink-oink! Neigh! MOOOO!"

Hound heard with alarm.

He turned and ran
to the old red barn.

Hound found his friends

all looking up.

He held his breath

when he saw Pup.

Pup backed up,

spilling feed and grain.

It poured with a *whoosh*

like a warm spring rain.

A feast for all

was at their feet.

Hooray for Pup!

An afternoon treat!

What a good Pup!

Look what he'd done.

Everyone was glad ...

123

... except maybe one!

Pup and Hound
Play Copycats

What was that?

An old leather shoe!

Pup pulled it away.

He wanted it, too.

So Hound chased the ducks

quacking their song.

Pup dropped the shoe,

then tagged along.

Hound stopped to visit

the pigs eating slops.

Pup pushed in, too,

smacking his chops.

Hound needed a nap —

a short getaway.

But that tagalong pup

wanted to play.

Hound hid by a tree.

Pup did, too.

Hound hid in a bush.

Pup did, too.

Hound went through the gate.

"Woof!"

Pup did the same.

Poor Hound was tired

of playing this game.

Hound ran to the corn maze
as fast as he could.

If that didn't work,

then nothing would!

Ah! Alone at last.

"Arf!" Not so fast!

Humph! Hound stomped

off to a stream.

He crossed the log —

a high balance beam.

Of course, that pup followed.

Go back, silly dog!

Pup's legs were wobbly,

and so was the log.

Whoopsy! Pup slipped!

He fell — *ker-PLUNK!*

Hound woofed when he saw

poor Pup get dunked.

Hound leaped in
and pulled Pup out.

He licked poor Pup

on his soft, wet snout.

Pup licked his wet fur.

And Hound did, too.

Then Pup smelled dinner.

And Hound did, too.

Pup trotted home.

Time for some chow.

Guess who followed?

Hound's the copycat now!

Pup and Hound
Hatch an Egg

What was that?

"Oink-oink! Moo! Neigh!"

What was the fuss?

Oh, look! A birthday!

A new baby filly

stood in the straw —

the wobbliest baby

Pup ever saw!

That spring, more babies
were born each week.
Baby songs rang out:

"Mew!"

"Baa!"

"Peep!"

"Squeak!"

Pup wanted to play.

The mothers said no.

Their babies were little
and needed to grow.

Pup went to the woods
with a hangdog pout.
Hound licked his fur
and kissed his snout.

Pup sat in the grass.

And there by his leg,

he found something round.

Pup found an egg!

Hound knew what to do.

Off to the lake!

Pup rolled the egg gently

so it wouldn't break.

They took it to Duck.

She cried, "Quack! Quack!"

That egg wasn't hers,

so Pup took it back.

Pup pushed the egg

past the pig's pen.

They went up the hill

to old Mother Hen.

But Mother Hen cried,

"Cluck-cluck! Bawk-bawk!"

That egg wasn't hers,

she said with a squawk!

Mother Hen was busy.

She had hatching to do!

She climbed on her nest

and told them to shoo!

Pup rolled the egg

past bales of hay.

Then suddenly,

that egg got away!

Over the hilltop,

over the knoll,

the egg began

to roll and roll!

It rolled down …

and down …

faster and faster!

Oh, no! Watch out!

What a disaster!

The egg hit a bump

and flew high in the air.

Ducks, chicks and donkeys

all stopped to stare.

They'd never seen

an egg fly — not ever!

Birds flew, but eggs?

How strange! How clever!

Down, down it came

past a panicky jay ...

and *thump*!

It landed right in the hay.

"Woof!" Pup was glad.

And so was Hound!

They hugged their egg.

They snuggled around.

The egg made a noise.

The dogs jumped back.

The shell broke in two
with a *crickety-crack*!

It didn't quack

and it didn't cluck.

It wasn't a chick.

And it wasn't a duck.

It made no sound.

It sat blinking its eyes.

It was a turtle!

Surprise! Surprise!

Friends wanted to play.

Pup and Hound said no.

Their turtle was little

and needed to grow.

They watched him and worried

as good parents do.

Now where Pup and Hound go,

Turtle goes, too!